Dedicated To

Ethan, Maddie, Cayla, Frankie, Chloe and Cai.

Ernie's Big Red Nose

Mary Jess

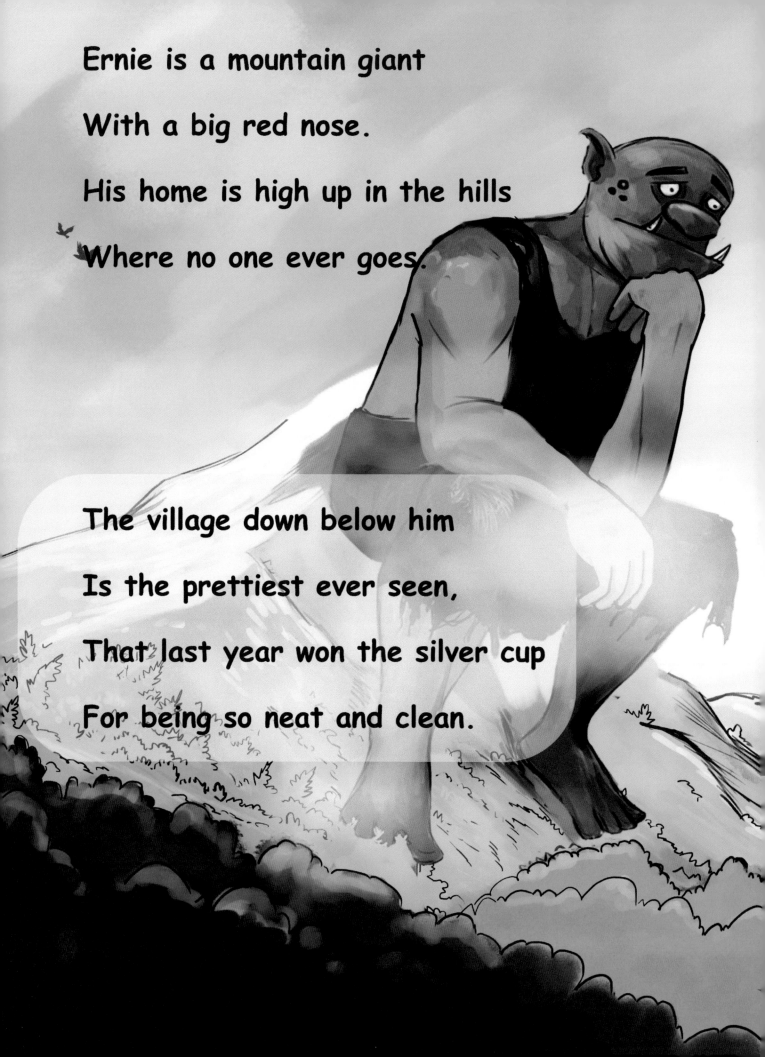

Ernie is a mountain giant

With a big red nose.

His home is high up in the hills

Where no one ever goes.

The village down below him

Is the prettiest ever seen,

That last year won the silver cup

For being so neat and clean.

Each sunrise Ernie's on his rock

For an hour or two,

Sitting down and contemplating

On his list of things to do.

One day he sneezed, green snot sprayed out,

His nose began to glow,

It glowed so bright the villagers

Could see it from below.

Ernie hadn't caused a problem

In the village all this time,

Until that day they woke

To find their village draped in slime.

It splattered every dog and cat,

It dripped from trees and roofs,

Like chewing gum it stuck

To Hannah's hair and Stephen's shoes.

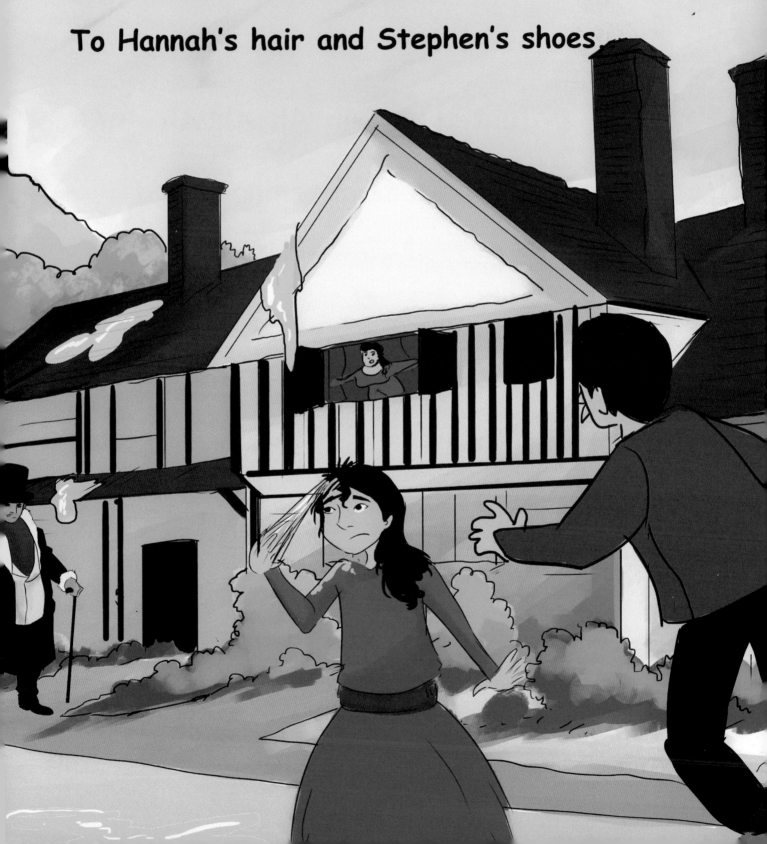

Just then "Ah Ah Ah Ah AhChoo!"

It was a frightening sound,

And everyone took cover

As more slime blew around.

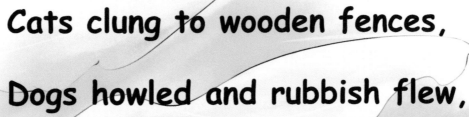

Cats clung to wooden fences,

Dogs howled and rubbish flew,

Tiles were ripped off rooftops

From the gust of the "AhChoo!"

You'll have to wash your hands with soap
So you don't catch my flu,

And make sure you isolate yourself
From others if you do."

They didn't follow this advice,

(If only they all knew!)

Soon each and every villager

Came down with Red Nose Flu.

They queued outside the doctor's

Hoping she would have a cure,

But how to cure this Red Nose Flu

The doctor wasn't sure.

The weeks passed by with Ernie

And the villagers still ill,

The weather turned much colder

And brought on a wintery chill.

Ernie's sneezes did not stop

But now his slime just froze,

And snowballs made of frozen snot

Fell from his big red nose.

This icy hail of snotballs

Was a danger there's no doubt,

Though children thought it fun

To kick the snotballs all about.

Adults loathed the frozen slime

That hung down from each roof,

And tripping over snotballs

Wasn't fun and that's the truth!

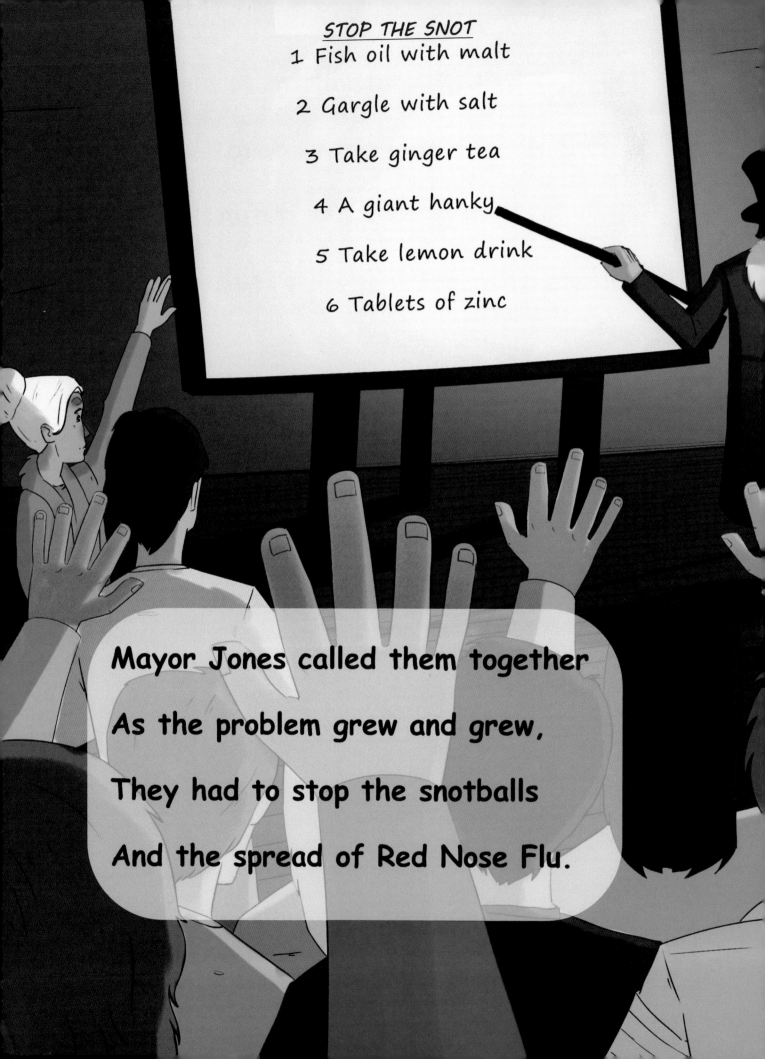

Each family brought two tablecloths,

Needles and some thread,

Mrs Jones said, "I will bring

Some tea with jam and bread."

"Ernie needs two," Rhian said,

"He's got to have a spare,"

When they gathered in the village hall

To have a sewing fayre.

He's going to need two!

They sewed the tablecloths together

Stitching them quite tight,

By breakfast time Mayor Jones declared,

"My word they look just right."

Two giant multicoloured hankies

Stretched across the floor.

"Now roll them both up carefully

And take them through the door."

A brass band played their favourite songs

And everyone joined in,

Ernie's voice above them moaned,

"Whatever is that din?"

"Ernie, look what we have made!"

They really had to yell,

"A hanky for your big red nose

And a spare as well."

Ernie tippy toed amongst

The people running round,

He didn't want to flatten

Anybody on the ground!

"We noticed that you never had
A hanky all this time,
And thought you'd find it useful
For your big red nose's slime."

"You've made them just for me?" he cried,
"You really are so good,
I can't get hankies big enough,
I only wish I could."

"You're very welcome Ernie
But do remember, PLEASE!
To use one of these hankies
Every time you need to sneeze."

Ernie took both hankies in his hands

And waved them all about,

Just then "Ah-Ah-Ah-Ah!" Oh no!

Another sneeze! WATCH OUT!

Ernie quickly held one hanky

To his big red nose in time,

"AhChoo! AhChoo!" THE HANKY WORKED!

And trapped the snotty slime.

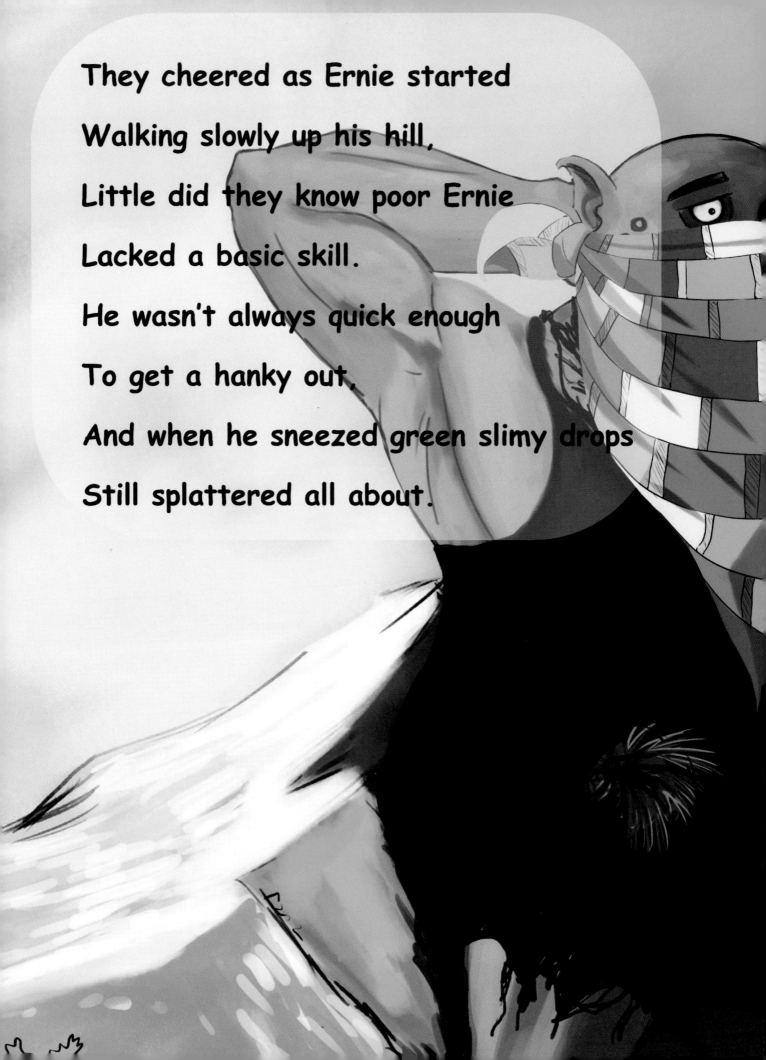

They cheered as Ernie started

Walking slowly up his hill,

Little did they know poor Ernie

Lacked a basic skill.

He wasn't always quick enough

To get a hanky out,

And when he sneezed green slimy drops

Still splattered all about.

Ernie was distraught to see

His green snot raining down,

He sat upon his favourite rock

His face creased in a frown.

"That's it!" he cried and quickly

Tied one hanky round his face,

With two big knots, the hanky-mask

Was safely held in place.

It worked so well to stop the spread

Of slime and Red Nose Flu,

The villagers decided that

They'd make some face masks too.

Then each and every person

Wore a mask upon their face,

And within two weeks the Red Nose Flu

Had gone and left no trace.

Normality returned

With people smiling every day,

But the Tidy Village Contest

Wasn't very far away.

So they organised some teams

That started cleaning up the mess,

Hoping that they would be able

To repeat last year's success.

High in the misty mountain

In the hills where no one goes,

A multicoloured face mask

Covers Ernie's big red nose.

Printed in Great Britain
by Amazon